I Call My Grandma
Gigi

Written by
Carole Aldred

Illustrated by
Trisha de Souza

I Call My Grandma Gigi
Copyright © 2021 by Carole Aldred

Tellwell Talent
www.tellwell.ca

ISBN
978-0-2288-6086-0 (Hardcover)
978-0-2288-6085-3 (Paperback)

To Carson, Emily, Oliver, Jacob, Harper & Marcus

I have a grandma I call Gigi.

She does yoga outside when it's not too breezy.

We love to hop on our bikes or follow the trails on our hikes.

And when we go to the beach, she wears a yellow bikini!

I have a grandma I call Grand-mère.

She says "Bonjour!" and dresses with flair.

She always has lots of treats for us to share,

And a cupboard full of toys and teddy bears.

I have a grandma I call Nonna.

She's usually in her kitchen cooking up pasta.

She makes her own dough and lets me help with the pizza.

And when the food is ready, she yells out "Mangia, Mangia"

I have a grandma I call Tutu.

She lives on an island in Honolulu.

She has a beautiful garden full of blooms.

We weave them together to make leis and crowns for our hair too.

I have a grandma I call Bibi.

She has a lot of books; some would say too many.

We spend hours reading on the sofa or under a tree.

And while we are reading, we sip chamomile tea.

I have a grandma I call Gramsie.

She lives on a farm with a garden full of veggies.

She has three apple trees and her very own bees.

With the apples we make pies; and gather honey from the hives.

I have a grandma I call Avo.

She cheers me on with "Bravo, Bravo"

On Sundays she makes a big family dinner.

Then we all dance around in the kitchen together!

I have a grandma I call Yaya.

She's very cool and eats papaya.

We love to paint and do all kinds of crafts.

Whenever we're together, we have so many laughs.

I have a grandma I call Nana.

We eat ice cream in a bowl topped with bananas.

We walk to the playground when the day is sunny.

Or stay inside for games if the day is rainy.

I have a grandma I call CeeCee.

She has a red sailboat and lives by the sea.

We pack sandwiches and cookies into a picnic basket.

Then off we go sailing and don't forget the life jackets!

I have a grandma I call Glamma.

We sip pink lemonade on her big veranda.

Sometimes she paints my nails in fun shades like Cherry Bliss.

And she smells like roses when she gives me a kiss.

A Grandma can be called many fun names.

But the love in her heart is always the same.

She loves to feed you and play your games.

And when it's time to go she says, "Come again!"

And no matter how big and tall you grow.

No matter where in life you go.

You'll always have a special place in her heart.

And you'll know she cares even when you're apart.

Author's note

Doing research for this little book was a lot of fun. In the end I had to cut out some of the names I had noted and chose a few for my book. Here are the meaning of the Grandmother names used.

Gigi: Ukrainian word for grandmothers it is widely used as a fun and easy way to address a grandmother. Can be an abbreviation of a name for example Grandma Gina becomes Gigi. Also used for great grandmothers. In French Gigi is a girl's name meaning "God is gracious".

Grand-mère: French word for grandmother. Since it is difficult for a toddler to pronounce it is often shortened to "mémé" or "mamère".

Nonna: Means grandmother in Italian and it is "bellisimo".

Bibi: Grandma in Swahili - a language spoken in some parts of Africa. Also used as a nickname for example Grandma Beth becomes Bibi.

Nana: An endearing term for grandmother commonly used since the two syllables make it easy for toddlers to pronounce.

Yaya: Also spelled Yia Yia means grandmother in Greek although it is so much fun whether you are Greek or not.

Tutu: Informal name for grandmother in Hawaiian. The formal term is kuku wahine. Tutu is used most commonly and for grandparents of both genders.

Gramsie: What my sister-in-law's grandchildren call her. Other similar popular nicknames include "Gammy" or "Grammy" or "Gaga".

Glamma: Meaning glamorous grandmother especially one who is relatively young or fashion conscious. It was first made popular by Hollywood actress Goldie Hawn.

Avó: Also Vavó are perfectly fitting for a Portuguese grandmother.

CeeCee: Also spelled Cici or Cece. A cool and trendy but less commonly used nickname for a grandmother.

I call my grandma

Draw or paste a picture of your grandma and what makes her special to you.

About the Author

An early riser, Carole starts her day with a walk along the shores of Lake Ontario and the picturesque Bronte marina near her home.

During the week she can be found in a courtroom where she works as a clerk and assistant to the judiciary in the Ontario Court of Justice.

She has always found joy and calm in creative pursuits such as music, writing, sketching and painting.

Most of all she cherishes every moment she can spend with her six grandchildren, reading, crafting and just watching them play.

She lives in Oakville, Ontario with her husband Chris. They spend their weekends together reading, gardening and escaping on adventurous road trips in search of quaint towns, beautiful nature trails and delicious food stops.

Find out more at www.whimsicalwords.ca

Illustrator Bio

Born in Dubai, Trisha de Souza (and her colouring pencils) immigrated to Canada when she was 5 years old. She began a career as a full-time artist in 2019. This is her first children's book. Trisha can be contacted at mademarionillustrated@gmail.com and her work can be found at www.mademarionillustrated.com

Made in the USA
Middletown, DE
22 July 2023

35571154R00020